# THE WORLD THROUGH DEXTER'S EYES

## The Foibles of a Too Big, Deaf Dalmatian and the Power of Love

Written by Vickie Versace Mullins

Photography by Megan V. Mullins

 FriesenPress

Suite 300 - 990 Fort St
Victoria, BC, V8V 3K2
Canada

www.friesenpress.com

ISBN
978-1-4602-8748-4 (Paperback)
978-1-4602-8749-1 (eBook)

*1. FICTION, FAMILY LIFE*

Distributed to the trade by The Ingram Book Company

# Table of Contents

This book is dedicated to

my mother, Margaret Versace, "Getta," and the abused
and unwanted animals that come into the world less
than perfect due to unethical breeding practices.

If you would like to know more about how to help
the animals, start with your local shelter.

Part of all profits will go to Dalmatian rescue,
local animal shelters and various animal charities.

# Chapter 1

## EARTH

In the beginning, it was silent, but there was so much more: shapes, objects, movement. Before, it was fluid, wet, and warm. We were cramped together like fish with fins, breathing in water. It felt good, and I was not alone. Then it was time; there came a flushing forth warm, a word became flesh, and my world was born.

Actually, if I know me, I sputtered out like an old-timey Ford that had quit for good and was ready for the junkyard. I was so big and part of a mistake litter. The foo-foos went for $1,000 each (to be trolloped out, again and again), but I was free. BAER (hearing) tested ended it all for me. A paper had to be signed, and I'd be the last of my kind. (Moan. Plop.)

The first thing I remember is running in all directions, going nowhere, oblivious to all around me. The others were the same,

1

running in oblivion, but soon it became apparent that I was different. I was the biggest, with one brown eye and one blue eye, but that wasn't all. *I was deaf.*

*Baby Dex*

We were all in different cages, but unlike the others, I was in mine more. I did get to go outside and play, but the number of playmates dwindled until there was no one left, not even one friend.

I found out later that, to put it nicely, I was about to be returned to where I came from. But Divine Providence intervened, and there appeared these big-hearted people who came for me, just in time. So glory be, I could begin my official purpose of being a dog and love and honor these philanthropists forever.

My humans: Mom, Dad, Megan and Granny (but I don't see her too much, she's in the home). We're called a family.

Like me, my dad is different. He is blind. I don't have ears, and he doesn't have eyes. That gave us an instant bond.

Then there's Megan. What can I say? I adore her. She enters the room, and I melt.

Next is Mom, who happens to be my inspiration for this written conglomeration. We communicate telepathically. For example, we go outside, and she pictures me doing my beeswax or lifting my leg. I do what she says through the brain waves if my stubbornness doesn't get in the way first or if the wires don't cross, which they often did. Then I do something backward, like bark the whole time I am *out* of my cage rather than in.

My mom says her spirit connected with mine before I was even born. She was yearning for another Dalmatian when she saw in the paper that there were some for sale. You don't see too many Dals anymore (except in shelters) because they have been so overbred, making them so hyper that nobody wants them. Well, she saw the ad and asked if she could come see them. She told the lady, straight up, that my dad wouldn't let her get another dog until my brothers passed. (That was why Mom wanted another dog—to ease the pain for when they did die.) Also, the other puppies were so expensive that she would never pay that price. This lady dog seller wasn't the most genteel; she was rather blunt. And with her seemingly impatient nature, why she let my mom and Megan come by twice was beyond me until she put her cards on the table.

"The little guy in the back is being put to sleep this Friday."

Mom said, "What guy?"

She said, "The deaf one."

Mom asked, "How much?"

She said, "Free."

"*Free?*"

"Yes, free."

Then Mom said, spreading out her arms as if she were in wonderland, "You mean a dog like these and free?"

Megan immediately said, "Wow, Mom, now I know why we're here."

But we had to talk to Dad first. He was at home. We had to convince him that it was the right thing to do, and when he heard that I was about to be put under, he gave in (reluctantly) right away. Actually, I think he instantly fell in love with me when we first met, as I jumped into his arms. So they put on my brand-new collar, with big bells so Dad would know where I was, and off we went into the sunset. (Later, when I was as big as a horse, there was no way Dad could miss me, but I still wore those bells because they had become my trademark.)

(By the way, nothing is ever free. With my antics, I cost the family a fortune in the end. But something had once happened to Mom that had made her promise herself that whenever possible, she would rescue a dog before she bought one from a breeder. She had seen a dog caught in a storm who needed her help, and she couldn't help him. And he died.)

4

At the kennel, my name was Larry. Could the people there have picked a dumber name? My brothers and sisters had names such as Champagne, Shar-pei, and Montana, to name a few. But mine was Larry, and that shows you what they thought of me. Well, when my people took me in, they gave me a *real* name: Dexter.

# Chapter 2

## COMING HOME

I hadn't asked to be on this earth, but I was meant to live. My strong will allowed it to be so. My family's kindness in saving my life was just a drop in the water—no bigger than a tear—but it was a start.

And oh, what a sacrifice I would turn out to be (especially for my sacrificial mom). I admit now that they sure had their hands full with me and still do. I was physically challenged by being deaf and thus would be challenging. I was labeled a "special needs" dog. I couldn't hear commands. I didn't make eye contact. I didn't understand. One of Mom's facial expressions (which I eventually learned to be "No!") scared me at first; her eyes and mouth were wide open. *Things will get better,* I told myself. *I promise. I will make it better!* It did get better as I slowly but surely outgrew those puppy brains of mine. And I truly didn't mean to hurt my family in any way. After all, a true sin is based on intent.

Part of my unruliness wasn't my fault. My brothers, Domino and Dice, were sick and dying when I arrived. They were both on pedestals due to being well bred, so they were hard acts to follow. With Domino being so sick, normally docile Dice was Alpha and did not like me. He bit my ear. I fell into a pool of stress. That home was, at the time, a nursing home for dogs—a sad home with lots of yelling. It's a miracle I didn't despair. But these people were so good that I was able to see beyond the grayness all around them. I knew instantly my purpose was to make them laugh.

Right from the start, my mom said I was clever. (But she admits now that she knew we were in trouble when I would not drink out of a water bowl but only out of the hose outside. She wondered what we would do in winter.) At three months old, I couldn't go down the stairs, but that didn't stop me. I glided down, like a tadpole that was almost a frog, dragging my back legs. And my barks were all different. Like a baby whose hunger cry is different from his wet cry, I had my anxiety cry and my piddle one, and my deep, low bark was my you-know-what cry. You know how dogs have accidents in their cages? Not me. I figured out early how to have the best of both worlds. Afghan intact, I would lift my leg and aim my squirt to go *outside* the cage, on the kitchen floor. (We had the most immaculate kitchen floor in the world because my mom was always scrubbing it!) My bed, with its covers, stayed warm and welcoming at all times because when nature called, I did my discreet thing. When it comes to den cleanliness, I'm your man!

I lived to play. At first my bounciness was cute as I plopped myself here and there. But when I got to be 80 pounds (eventually 120!)

of all muscle, jumping around and landing in laps wasn't too cool anymore. (When I got to be about 100 plus pounds, I went on the "Choose to Lose" program at the vet. I lost 10 pounds, but then, typical dieter that I was, I gained it back.)

I didn't like the car or walks. (Down the road, I learned to like them a bit, at least the car rides.) In the beginning, both activities seemed to exacerbate my already hyper condition. My future began to look as if I would be confined to the kitchen and living room, as well as outside in my fenced playground. (My play area was all concrete rather than grass, so when I was lucky enough to get grass later, it was a real luxury, considering that I think most everyone takes grass for granted. Rolling around in the grass: There's nothing like it.) So that wasn't too bad, in the scheme of things. At least I was alive.

The reason I later began to like the car was that the rides eventually blossomed into going to the doggie park, where I could expand my horizons immensely—and run and run (in the grass)! You could literally see the joy on my face as I ran with my big tongue hanging out, flapping to the side in the wind.

"Look at the Dalmatian!"

"Come on, Spot!"

I could see the wonder on people's faces as they called and pointed! Their excitement made me wish that I could jump through hoops for them. Kids wanted their pictures taken with me. But I also became known as the notorious dog who lifted his leg on anyone I took a particular fancy to. I liked them so much that I just couldn't contain myself! I had to mark my turf where I was, at the moment, so happy. And if I saw a particularly crowded area—like a bunch of people sitting around a picnic table—you guessed it. Being the social butterfly that I was, that's the first place I headed. After all, I was among friends. Mom thought that if anyone wanted to take me home with them, I would go. By the gate, longingly watching them leave, whimpering. But I would never do that!

I was bad, so full of mischief. I appeared not to be trainable. (The first and last trainer I had died young, after working with me. No, not really because of me . . . I don't think.) Well, I eventually got somewhat trained, but, like Frank Sinatra, *I did it my way.* I couldn't be walked without pulling an arm off, unless I had on my Gentle Leader. Then I did a slow prance. I was so curious that my mouth went around everything. (Love those bottles of water in the fridge!) Incidentally, and I don't mean to brag, but I opened the refrigerator myself.

I began to explore every part of the house. I was a one-dog demo-lition crew. When I got nervous (which was often as I was later diagnosed with an anxiety disorder and given Prozac), I would eat the siding on the house, or whatever I had a particular taste for. Once we were all sitting down to watch television and nothing happened. But my dad immediately figured out why, and he was spot on (pun intended) as he went outside and discovered I had chewed the cable wires. Next were his Bose headphones, *two times* with *two different pairs.* (To quote Shakespeare, "That way madness lies.") I'd say the headphones just weren't meant to be. Dad's breathing equipment hose was next. I left my mark on the wooden chairs on the patio, too—not a "Dexter was here" mark, but chewing up all the arms. Well, you get the idea. Before I came along, the side screen door (another thing I pushed over the edge with my destructiveness) was old, but after me, it was done. The hinges were rusted, so I went in and out as I pleased. No such thing with the new door. I had to be let in and out. It was just another trial for a dog who couldn't understand boundaries.

Some visitors called me "Devil Dog." But who wouldn't think that, with my blue eye often staring, like a wolf does, showing off my wild side? Or Mom would say I was deaf, and others would look at my funny eyes and immediately shake their heads knowingly, actually thinking I was blind.

All in all, though, my loved ones hardly ever got angry with me or gave up on me. (Maybe they got mad with themselves but never with me.) And it was a good thing because I don't think anyone else would have had me with my bad habits and all, other than the Sunshine Farm where I could live out the rest of my life.

Actually, I could have been adopted out again to make someone else's life hard.

I sampled, tasted, devoured. When I was done chewing, I was done exploring. It really was not my fault that shoddy workmanship seems standard these days.

Along the way, Mom made a few casual jokes about me that I didn't think were too funny. But I shouldn't have taken them too seriously because, as I've mentioned, my family loves me. I think she actually did it for comic relief with me, the jester. She would ask a repairman:

"Want a dog for $100?"

And he would answer, "Oh no, not even if he was free. I don't have enough room for a dog."

Mom would then clarify herself: "No, I would *give* you $100 if you take him."

One day at the vet with Izzie—you will meet her later—the vet commented on her tag, which read "Big Reward." Well, mine didn't say that. Mom told the doctor that it wasn't necessary because the minute someone found me, they would quickly return me after they saw what they was dealing with. (Tear!) Ah, life. It is so bittersweet at times. But my owners seemed to love me unconditionally, and it is true that love can't hear or see.

Mom got so frustrated with me at one point that she contacted a dog whisperer. She told the lady everything that was going on, such as why she couldn't even tiptoe by my cage without me waking up. And she needed a break from me once in a while! Well, the lady told Mom, in a past life, I was tied outside and killed in a storm, and when I didn't see my family on the other side, I grabbed the first body earthbound, which was a Dalmatian with many afflictions. That sounded a little familiar to Mom, but she couldn't place it—at least in this life. The lady said I could use some Reiki, too, and she was going to come over and give it to me for free. *Free?* Yes, free. We'll see!

Finally, after many tribulations, one event shed a lot of light on my situation. I developed a deep sore that literally turned into a hole on my head, which my mom thought was a brain tumor and my dad thought was nothing. (They never agreed on anything, so when they finally came to a compromise, it was, like always, my mom's way.) So they took me to this special vet who said, "This guy isn't just deaf, but he is a cretin." A *what?* "Cretin" is an old-fashioned word that means big and dumb, usually due to a congenital thyroid condition. And that was why I couldn't learn. Well, by then I already knew that I was not dumb, and I was tired of others thinking that. Eccentric, maybe, but not dumb. Stupid, but not dumb. *Deaf,* but not dumb. I bark a lot.

He said that he had never seen such a sore, and I thought I had never seen such a vet. Well, the blood work came back fairly normal but showed a *very* bad yeast infection that was also in my ears and toes, which made them hurt terribly. No wonder I cried half the night in my cage. Thus, I was redeemed somewhat (*hmm, cretin, grr*) and labeled just an ordinary dog. Phew. And then he said that I was big (attitude immediately changing)—one of the biggest boys he had ever seen. For a Dal. And good looking. And hyper. With one brown eye and one blue, and a head up in the clouds, right off the planet Neptune, and too smart. If there was ever such a thing as ADHD in a dog, I had it. (We had switched vets over that one. My mom had suspected ADHD, but one vet had said that there was no such thing, just bad behaviors—tsk, tsk, tsk.)

I was so different. I actually turned on the stove and the oven with my big paws. The fridge door had to be taped as I got older. I would just help myself. I could choose to have something, or not. (I eventually got the tape from the drawer and got rid of it for good.)

I'd sit on the couch and watch TV. If I saw friends on the screen, I would get all excited, running back and forth from the dining room window to the front one. I'd kind of jump up onto the

big-screen TV and almost knock it over when I saw a dog. Meg said that would be a good commercial for a big-screen, high-definition TV. When I got tired, which happened only after I was totally worn out from physical and mental activity, I lay my head on the back of the couch, looking out, sighing wistfully, and dreaming of playing. Then my head would droop, and I was almost out, and Mom knew it was bedtime.

I would sit at the kitchen table, chair pulled slightly out. I invented this move myself, but Mom took it further. She motioned for me to get on the chair and made us a bagel. (This worked great until I became ill with a kidney stone and had to be put on a special diet. Then she wondered why I couldn't stop hounding her for bagels.) She put out her hand for me to stay. If I got down, I had to get back up. When we shared our food, I had to sit like a

gentleman. We shook hands and paws. If I barked, she would go "Shh" and blow on my nose, but sometimes it was okay, like when she signed, "Speak!" When we were done, she made her hands go up and down in the air, saying, "All gone."

I often sat in that chair, looking way up and all around so I wouldn't miss a thing. And I yawned, with my head back straight up. All those times Megan was ready with the camera to get my unusual poses.

*The Second Most Beautiful Dog in Euclid, Ohio*

If nothing else, I was photogenic. (The city's animal shelter had a contest, and I was voted the second most beautiful dog in Euclid, Ohio. I was also Mr. July in the calendar. The foo-foos weren't the only ones who were show quality.)

It was fun to drink out of my own water fountain (the hose) and even a bottle of water, if it was in someone else's mouth first. Once I found a bottle of water, took the cap off (somehow positioning it just right), and got myself some water. When I couldn't get any more out and the water was emptied all over the place, I made a toy out of the bottle and kept shaking it. My dad said I was something else. Wired differently, I certainly was. (Touch me and watch me sizzle.)

I made peace with my spray bottle (which I was often spray-knocked with when I was naughty) by wanting it sprayed in my mouth, like a squirt gun. But if I didn't listen, that same bottle was used as a punishment tool. (Mom also used the bottle to spray and scrunch her hair to create curls.) I learned to distinguish the different uses of that bottle.

I was so dutiful at times. When I couldn't eat my full bowl of food, which was nuggets with warm water (I like my meals hot!) I'd leave a perfect half, like half of a pie. Or when I did my business, I went only in certain places so as not to ruin any of my play area. Mom said all of that was a sign of brilliance or autism. All these compliments made for a swollen head.

I took on the different moods of the house. That's what a good dog often does, though it is not necessarily right. Someone must be strong! But empathy kicks in, and we take on the illnesses and problems of our owners to lighten their loads. Why, I would bite for them! (My late brother Domino had done just that. He was then incarcerated, which consisted of having to be in his cage whenever people came over, especially kids. He cost my parents a fortune. Thank goodness for homeowners insurance.)

I would lie on top of my dad's belly, on my back, showing all my parts. (I also do that when I am having REM sleep.) That would practically stop my dad's breathing, but I was so cute, who could resist? Now, if I could just refrain from doing that to Mom or Meg.

Basically I am sweet but tough. I would put my bone in my dad's face so he knew I was there to play. He held it like a baby bottle. Engrossed in my chewing, I'd give him little ear nibbles. We Dals are noted for that: nibbling on ears (sometimes jumping up to do so and scaring the liver out of people) and leaning, attached to our owners like Velcro.

Ahh. Sometimes I wonder if I am a person acting like a dog or a dog acting like a person. How many dogs do you know who write books?

By this time, my mom had taught me more tricks: how to sit, sit up, get down and lie on the floor, give my paw. She put on my leash in the house, which further helped me behave. It all civilized me. It seems to me after that, I had to earn everything. She sometimes signed to me: "I love you." "Calm." "Go outside," with those fingers "walking" across the palm. "Come here." A shaking head, meaning "No!" The "time out" signal changed to mean "Come on and get a treat!" When it was dark outside, flicking the light on and off meant to come in. My favorite game: Get a touch of the moonlight, go potty, flashlight shined on me, get a treat. (They clicker train dogs now. Say a command, click, say good boy, treat. But for me it was flicker training.)

Nonetheless, my mom mostly "talked" to me, all the time, never shutting up, with those Italian hands, and her big eyes and mouth, and I understood a lot. She and I were almost constant companions, and everything was touch. She couldn't walk by me without skimming her hand across my body as if it were silk. She often counted my spots. They call it the language of love. I grew so tied to the woman that I couldn't do anything without looking at her first for approval. I worried a lot about her leaving me.

I was a creature of habit. I had the same routine every day, or I'd go nutty. That happened a lot because I lived with a busy family. In some ways, though, I had it down pat. I knew that when my dad watched me, anything went. He was the most fun. Megan's presence turned me into a wet noodle. She was just too cute—my good one. And Mom was the boss. (For as lenient as she was, she was also strict.) She had the patience of a saint; St. Francis of Assisi could not have done a better job. She was even saintlier when she got up a couple times a night to let me outside to use the restroom. She found out that it was best not to let anything throw me off too much as I was already imbalanced because I couldn't hear.

When the barometer dropped, I got especially loopy. I acted like a maniac because when that happened, often the wind would kick up, followed by thunder (I can *feel* the thunder) and next would come a storm. So if the barometer changed, I automatically went into storm mode. I don't like rain (that's why I look up to the sky and bark at it) and storms scare me. But life isn't always pretty.

My mom went above and beyond. I had not a toy box or a boom box, but a *bone* box! And just about every morning, she gave me a treasure hunt in my cage—a big mistake. It made me more spoiled, if that's possible. A dog biscuit, peanut butter, or a different treat in my Kong every day. A Jumbone. (I'm licking my chops now, just thinking of one of those.) Anything to keep my chewing of the furniture down to a limit and my mind busy. I could down one-hour bones in twenty minutes! I thought her

hunts were so admirable until I realized there was a method to her madness. She would go up to bed and sneak a nap for a couple hours more on those early, cold mornings! But not for long: As soon as I figured out it was really daytime, after I finished my treats and snoozed a bit myself, the anxiety would engulf me; I thought of the silence in the night, and I knew I had to *get out of this cage*. But Mom played a quick one on me, even then. If I barked and barked, it prolonged my time in the cage. If I waited patiently, I got out sooner. I hated my cage so much (hmm, dog's den—yeah right) that when I had to be in it (mostly when my family left the house), my mom would give me treats to lure me inside. The treats became more and more exotic as I would not barter for less. Dog trainers would *never* agree with this method. It could have been easier if Mom would have learned *regular* sign language and forced me to be trained. But a deaf puppy is very overwhelming to begin with, so I guess she did her best. Thus, Mom and I rewrote the textbook, and I turned out all right. (Hmm, we'll have to discuss that later.)

Some would say that when I got older, I became neurotic. Once I went to a vet who had leather collars and leashes hanging on hooks on the wall in the exam room. Well, I acted like an animal and went crazy—literally climbing walls to get at them. Nobody could handle me. Well, what do you expect under the circumstances?

Maybe it was Mom who was the real neurotic for taking me to such a vet.

Now that you know my background, I am free to tell some stories!(A story that never ends . . . so we'll do another chapter and begin again.)

# Chapter 3

## MY BROTHERS

Though in heaven, it wouldn't be right if I didn't dedicate a short chapter to my brothers Domino and Dice. They communicate with me now more than they did in the land of the living.

I love them, but we weren't together for very long. Domino was too sick to play; Dice didn't understand, and I couldn't hear. Dice was mad at me all the time because I kept mixing up who was the boss, and he wasn't the type to get mad. Domino was always the head honcho until he got so sick, then Dice took over. Dice wasn't in the best of health to do the job properly either, so I tended to take over, but no way would Dice let that happen. When he bit my ear, he drew blood.

Domino was the neat one, the Felix Unger of this odd couple, and Dice, the show dog, the slobberer, was Oscar Madison. The family often called him Mr. Deuce because they got him second. Domino always licked Dice clean, especially after Dice got into the garbage. (The show dog!)

Domino always took care of Dice. One time Domino came into the house, all out of breath and barking as if something were very wrong, so Mom went outside and found that Dice had escaped outside the fence and was in the neighbor's yard. When Dice was neutered, the vet said to put him and Domino in separate cages that night (they shared a cage). Well, Dad didn't do that, and Mom was nervous. Waking up in the middle of the night, Mom saw Domino's "arm" around Dice. Aw. They used to get loose and run all around, sometimes during a bad snowstorm (they became snow dogs), and then Mom would catch Dice, the good boy, and Domino would come running.

It seemed like whatever those two did, Domino was in the driver's seat, with Dice right by his side. I'm sure they must have had many other lives together before they came here. Domino often shared these stories with me because he often came to visit me from the spirit world. Mom knew when this happened because I would look startled and then shake my ears in response to nobody there. Domino looked out for me.

Domino passed first, then it was Dice's turn about five months later. The problem with Dice's passing was that he still had presence of mind (well Domino did too), but his body was so tired. Mom and Dad took Dice for French fries right before they went to the vet. They were crying at the drive-through window of McDonald's. They had to explain what was happening to the girl. Dice ate the fries as always. At the vet, Dad stayed in the car sobbing, and Mom went in, sitting with him on the floor because he was too big for the stainless steel table—his head looking up, taking his last breath, resting on her heart. That would soothe her grief.

My mom never went into the room with any of her other animals when they were being put to sleep. But Dice was different. He never asked for anything. She felt she owed it to him. Domino was always asking and getting what he wanted, the spoiled one. (Actually, Domino was downright bad sometimes; once he ate rocks.) But Dice was gentle and meek. He was mostly Dad's dog, but he deeply loved Mom. Same thing with Domino: Domino was Mom's boy, but he dearly loved Dad. There you have it.

You're beacons of light that have grown dim. We hope to see you again, amen.

*Domino and Showboat Dice*

Mom saw Domino after he passed, on the other side of the fence. She asked him why he was on the wrong side of the fence, and he said because now he was on the other side.

# Chapter 4

## LOVE

One day, Mom and Megan introduced me to the beach. I saw this big bowl of water and began to drink from it, thinking it was all mine. But then I saw others around, and I knew I had to share. Being an only dog, I often think the sun shines on me, and it does, but it shines on everybody else, too. On the positive side, though, we are never alone because of this connection in life.

I stood proudly on the sand like a stallion, ears blowing back with the wind, waves crashing in. It put me in another world, and I thought to myself, *Ah, I love water*. From that point on, I have been drawn to water. Words cannot adequately explain how I feel about water. I love waterfalls, oceans, and streams. In my dreams, I fall asleep on a limb over water, looking down on dark blue, titanic waters, with stars in the sky. Then, an extra big wave comes up, and I run for my life and remember from some distant memory, *I am afraid of drowning!* So much for that.

On summer nights, I like to play outside under the stars, catching some night air and seeing all the doggie spirits up there in the Animal Kingdom of Heaven. The lightning bugs uplift me because they remind me that we are all beings of light. In the winter, I frolic with the snowflakes and eat an imaginary snow cone to refresh me. The flakes are like Christmas ornaments. Mom thinks that I'm funny because there is nobody out there to play with, but I am acting as if there is. I see my special angels, my spirit guides: Dice, all innocent, who had the face of God, and Domino, smiling and looking dapper. On the earth he was a handsome devil! I see them in the clouds. If nothing else, these images are my imaginary playmates, which is also common for an only dog.

I pray: Here is some love being sent to you, my brothers, my ancestors, and all who came before me and paved the way for this day. Amen.

May they rest in peace.

It was a sleepy June day. Outside I jumped into a plastic chair, it flipped over, and the next thing I knew, I was intertwined in it. I tried to get out and couldn't. So I thought, *What can I do?* I stayed calm, and soon my mom came out and tried to rescue me. She said that with my head down and my tail between my legs, I had the sweetest, most surrendering look on my face. She couldn't untangle me, so she called my dad, and he completed the rescue mission of love. Later, I turned the chair over and urinated on it.

I'm the kind of dog who likes to always be in someone's back pocket. Sometimes I can't tell where my family ends and I begin—and I like it that way. If you don't like a dog who is attached to your hip, you don't need a spotted one like me. I'm the type of dog who will open my heart to you. I love to be loved all day long, and I give lots of kisses back. "Love licks," I call them. If I can't impart a kiss on you, I will flap my tongue, like I do when I have peanut butter in my mouth.

In the living room once, I was lying on the love seat, and Megan sat on the couch. I jumped down, gave her a lick, and then went back to my place. If my mom is doing something like the dishes, I lean against her leg. If she bends over, my head rests on her behind. When my mom is with me, she can't do as much work as usual because I need her undivided attention. She dusts a table, I pucker, she kisses me, and she dusts again. That's our rhythm. I actually center and relax her, and Megan calms me. Sometimes I turn into *two* wet noodles when she walks in the room. Oh, love's magic . . .

The other day I was looking at myself in the mirror. I'm a pretty handsome boy, made in the image and likeness of God. Do you know that there is no other Dalmatian in the world like me? Well, that is true for all beings and nature. No two birds are alike. No two trees. No two Megans. Not even identical twins (they don't come out together; one goes first). No two dogs are alike, spotted or otherwise. Our masters are our closest experience to God. By the same token, dogs are meant to light their way and make their lives brighter, whether or not they are spotted wonders. Here is the absolute truth: That is why *all* dogs are all gods, spelled backward! (It sounds blasphemous, but it is true.) And all dogs go to heaven.

The pupil in my eye is sort of star shaped. A starfish, a genetic anomaly. It's probably another unusual connection to being deaf, but my mother says it is like a beauty mark. My family thinks it is just something else that makes me special, just like the heart-shaped spot on my nose.

Love has no flaws. Love is ancient, love is blind. It does not envy, it does not boast, it is not loud. It does not dishonor others, it is not . . . err, I got a little carried away there!

Love can make hearts come out of nowhere! After Granny died, Meg and Mom saw hearts everywhere they looked. In a house often filled with *conditional* love, toward me it was always unconditional. I was here to teach more than one lesson.

They say you begin to mature when you can accept yourself for who you are. That means loving yourself. Be good and take care of yourself—that is the beginning of it all. Self-love one day branches out to the love of others. You can't be loved or happy unless you love yourself first. Then there's the higher form of love, *agape*—the spiritual, humanitarian love. Self-love, not selfish love. I am working on that, but I have a ways to go.

"*Namaste*. The God in me salutes the God in you." "Self-actualization" is a fancy term for finding yourself. Again, I'm not talking about selfish love, but the love in which you love the God inside you, Who resides in everyone and even in nature. The Higher Self. "Love thy neighbor as thyself."

When you love your spot, no matter how dark it is, you can move onto something better. But first you have to be thankful for what you have and where you are because something more intelligent than all of us put together has guided you there, so you are exactly where you are supposed to be.

How do I know all this? Maybe I was a human once, or maybe I will be one the next time around.

My happiest times were when my family was together watching movies and I was gnawing on a big bone. It was love personified. I didn't feel complete if Megan was upstairs. So I'd run up, open the door to her room, and steal her Strega Nona doll or her moose, given by a friend who had had it made just for her and to look just like her, eyeglasses and all. I eventually chewed it up for good, and Strega Nona was finished, too. At times I was such a bad guy.

Megan cried. That got her attention right away, but it was negative attention.

Once I got Megan's big, stuffed Saint Bernard dog, a real childhood relic and almost bigger than me, if you can believe that. Well, I dragged it into my cage and chewed it to pieces. When my mom saw me, it looked as if I were in a tub full of soap suds. She didn't know if she should laugh or what. Boy, was that hard to clean up! My Megan cried again and again. (Love can hurt!) Never would she find another stuffed dog like that. I don't know why I did such things.

But guess what? Again something intervened. When Meg was sick, Mom went into the drugstore to buy some medicine, and there was another stuffed Saint Bernard, priced reasonably. Only one was left, and it was much softer. Meg cuddled with it in her bed, and then being sick wasn't so bad. (She got a pink elephant once, too. But you know what? I never touched it!)

The stuffed Dalmatian that looked just like me had a similar fate. I got it and ripped it, and it was done. Wasn't one of me enough? But come Christmas, there was a miracle, as always, because Mom had found another one. Someone was looking out for them. They have the real thing here, so why do they need a stuffed one? Humans can be greedy.

I always want Megan to be a part of our quality time together, even though my dad is my left hand and my mom is my right, both seeing for me what I cannot hear. (Except Dad!) I don't know what I will do when Megan goes away to college. But we will always be connected—all of us together, our own circle of life. We allow others into our circle when we have company. I so love it when we have visitors because I am a people dog.

If my humans were preoccupied during family time and not paying much attention to me, I'd get a sock and shake it in their faces so they could focus back on me. If that didn't work, I'd swallow it.

Once when the television was broken, I stood in front of it so they could just watch me. Why, I'm a wonder dog, and Mom often says that I am lucky not to be dead from all my doings. Candy wrappers made of foil that I'd get out of the garbage went straight into my mouth. One time I ate a pack of gum (which is supposed to be poisonous to dogs) and dreamed of blowing bubbles out of both ends.

Later on, my sock-eating habit became something I enjoyed more than just annoying my family. Many times I was sick, and once I threw up one sock and passed the other one out the back end. Mom, Dad, and Meg couldn't put on a pair of socks without me salivating. To this day I have a problem with socks. (I need to attend Sox Anonymous.)

My new favorites became underwear and Meg's hairbands, and once I even tried to eat Mom's nightgown. I put a corner of it in my mouth, heaved it in, but I couldn't get the rest in because it was so big. Mom sternly pulled it out of my mouth. I never tried that again because my mom got angry. And *watch out* when she gets mad! Plus I didn't like the hydrogen peroxide that was often given to me to ingest so the sock would come right out before reaching mid-gut.

Once I had a horrible stomachache. I had had two other ones like it before, but this one was the worst. The last two, within a couple of weeks, had gone away after two big globs of something nasty came out of me. What were *those?* Dishrags! So palatable. But this time, I had eaten a pair of socks, too (big feet, big socks), and after several days, they hadn't come up. Mom said that if I didn't pass them, I would have to go to the hospital and have an operation. A different owner would take me home because she would be through.

Well, I ended up at the emergency vet with $200 worth of X-rays and an enema (which caused my stomach to hurt more), and Mom wouldn't talk to me. I must say, though, the girl who gave me the enema was very gentle and never hurt me once.

That's what you call a good girl.

My mom left one day. She didn't hug me good-bye; she had a bunch of bags. She waved at me, and I looked behind me to see who she was waving at. I thought her face looked funny and she was leaving me forever. My insecurity was again rearing its ugly head. But she came back the next night. A week later, I saw her leave again. She had a big smile on her face. This time she hugged and kissed me. She had on a straw hat and a light blue blouse with big white flowers. I learned later that she was going to Florida with Meg and Binh (you'll eventually meet him). She didn't come back for a while, but I remembered that kiss and that she did come back to me before, so she would be back again. Plus I was with my dad, family friends Bob, and Don, and I had a good time, bonding with the guys.

When my mom came home, she said I looked all relaxed and cared for. I got a bone, threw it up in the air, and ran back and forth in the house. I jumped all up and down for joy and thought of how I am happy and love my family and people. All was good.

Later, at the new house, sometimes I slept with Dad upstairs in the big bed. Other times, I slept with my mom. I'm Mama's dog, but I am fair to Dad, too. I'm not like Izzie (you will meet her soon, I promise), who was Dad's girl 24/7. She wanted Mom or Megan only when Dad wasn't there. Two-faced, I think you call it. Yet she became Mom's dog, too, and slept all the time with her. (She still followed Dad all around, though, watching him.) And she snoozed with the big Dex—me! That's what you call a full house, err, bed.

# Chapter 5

## SNOOPY AND SPOTTED DOGS

Snoopy is a philosopher, like I am. He is a celebrity from Mom's time, and she told me about him because I reminded her of him. After I heard about him, I thought he was pretty slick, so now I always strive to be like him. He is my idol. I'd probably be on my back, looking at the stars, on the roof of my doghouse, too, if I had one.

Why, I also think I look a little like him. Looking in the mirror, pushing my ears back, smiling widely to show my big teeth, I think I definitely look like Snoopy. What do you think? Maybe I resemble a side view of him, or his *silhouette*, with a cheesy smile.

I learned to leer like Snoopy, too. I just lean my head down, lower it some more, and stare one of those cool stares—as if I am trying to figure you out. (When Megan's with her dates, I do that and then get between them.) Scary! I guess you can say that I was definitely a dog with too much time on my hands, err, paws.

Snoopy is an ageless cartoon character, made in the likeness of a real dog. I don't know if he represents someone great who already walked the face of this earth or if he came right from the drawing board, from an original idea. He sure seems real, though.

If he were real, we would be related. In God's eyes, we would be related! And maybe he would have been with Adam and Eve, our first parents, if they had a dog. Then he would be the first dog. (Just like the White House sometimes has a First Dog.) Then many dogs would come from *The Dog*, the *One Dog*. Not a guide dog, or a guard dog, but a god dog.

My mom did say it was a spotted dog who introduced her to reading in the first grade. *See Spot Run*, a best seller from way back when, at least defined the spotted dog, which makes me think spotted dogs *were* the first dogs to inhabit the earth. And after that, mutations occurred, and there began the official world of dogs! But no matter, a dog is a dog is a dog.

Many say the Dalmatians are from the beautiful Dalmatia in Croatia. I don't know if that is true. I don't know if they got their name from Dalmatia, or if Dalmatia got its name from them. (Just imagine a dog breed so great that a place was named after them!)

Here is something to consider: If you *feel* something is true, then it is the truth, and it is real. It may not be the same truth another being feels, but it still has authenticity. For example, if you say the sky is green, who am I to say it is not green? (Hey, are you color-blind? I am.) Anyway, what I just said about the Dalmatians may not be true, but now I am going to give you some facts.

Did you know Dalmatians are born white and "grow" their spots as they get a little older? It is a recessive gene that makes this so, which is why so many Dals are deaf, have two different colored eyes, or just have blue eyes, or even green eyes. They often have sensitive skin. Dals are also known to be "stone makers," so they are highly prone to kidney infections and problems. (It is all of the above for me, sigh.) Thus they must eat foods low in protein and purines, although one vet said that either you are prone to stones and must eat that way or you are not.

After Disney's movie *101 Dalmatians* came out, everyone wanted a speckled pup with a red bow under the Christmas tree. But they didn't know anything about the breed. (Or that you should never bring a dog as a gift to a home during the chaos of a holiday!) They just jumped in and bought the Dal, but when the puppy got older and bigger, and they saw what raising it entailed, they weren't up to it. Many Dals ended up in shelters. Now, some people like what raising a Dalmatian entails, but others can't handle such a rambunctious breed, or any hyper dog.

We are big. We are strong. We need lots of exercise. We are service dogs. After all, why do you think we became the mascot for the fire department? Legend has it that we used to run beside fire trucks on their way to fires. We aren't sport dogs, although we look pretty sporty; we are a working breed. You know what I say: Let me work, oh let me work. The dog walker who helped us out a bit said that I needed a job, a purpose. So before I die, I hope I can be a therapy animal somewhere. I have to settle down first.

# Chapter 6

## WHAT'S IN A NAME?

This is embarrassing to admit, but my nickname used to be Poopy—or at least it was when I was a pup. Thank goodness, I eventually outgrew the name. The story goes that "poopy" was the only word I could "hear" when my mom's shrill voice called it: "Poopy! Poopy!" (I can "hear" trains, too, or at least feel their vibrations. And I can "hear" the vibes of loud music.) She must have really liked that name, probably because in potty training, I learned that part first; it was something you never did in the house (maybe once or twice in my then-short life did I go in the house). Outside, I was always so organized, going only in two different places. When we later moved to a house with grass, I defecated in a row so as not to mess up my play area and so I could wallow easier without getting smelly.

When I was first being housebroken, I had little accidents. When I did, my mom or dad simply let me out. They didn't say "Bad!" and hit my nose, or make much of a fuss. Some people put their dog's nose in the mess. But in one of the more modern training books, a dog is giving you a gift when he piddles in the house, which is the utmost in submission. Now if you put my nose in a mess, it not only hurts my dignity but also makes me want to give a bigger and better gift next time because you didn't appreciate my first one!

I was almost named Ace, Sugar, Sage, or (Baby) Beluga. Later on, I was called every variant of the name Goober: Goobalube, Goobaliscious, Goobalish, Goobarius, Mista Goob (Meg's favorite), and Goobie. Don't forget Decadent (Deckie), as in delicious but slightly evil, and Larry. Phew, no wonder I'm nuts! But Dexter is my official name, a Southern name, even though my kind is from across the pond. I am European, not Southern, but I will take it! And even though I am dorky, I am proud to have the name of a gentleman from the South. (I am a roughneck, not a redneck.) One more thing: Dextrose means sugar! Plus I'm very dexterous.

Mom sometimes liked to give her "kids'" at least the middle name of someone famous. Megan got the name of a soap opera star, Megan Victoria, though unintentionally. In order to call me Poopy, my mother had to justify it. So she gave me the middle name of "Shipoopi," which is a song in *The Music Man* about a girl being hard to get. (My girl will be hard to get because she will be special, but someday I will have one.)

Dexter Shipoopi Mullins, Poopy for short. I don't think there is another dog with that name. My family got me, named me, and *then* learned the etymology of the words. Yep. My family sure got it right.

# Chapter 7

## SOME TOUGH TIMES

Mom and I have telepathy, and recently I learned she got a speeding ticket. She watches for law enforcement, almost neurotically, when she's driving so she doesn't get a ticket and have to pay. (It ruins your driving record, too.) Well, apparently, she looked away this time, and with her defenses down, she got a ticket. How could that be? She had a car full of girls and was rushing them to a game, late as usual. She was doing something good. I say that getting a speeding ticket is like a roulette wheel. When it is your turn, then it is yours.

I helped Mom by ripping up the ticket—or I *thought* I was helping her. But she got *mad*. Cities need to get money in ways other than through taxes, so they make the speed limit 25 miles per hour, then switch it almost immediately to 35, and then back to 25. They want to confuse you. The cops are out there watching, and with one little slip, you owe $150 as if it's no big deal. Go to court and sit half a day, and you save only $25. They get you either way.

Then Mom got another ticket! It was bad timing. Those radars are the root of all evil. Why, nowadays you don't even need to get stopped. You get a citation in the mail, and you know then that they gotcha!

Have you ever received a ticket for going too slow? Well, Mom never got one, but she was stopped once and told the speed limit on the freeway was 60, or at least 55, not 20, so she had to go faster or get off the freeway. You can't win.

Mom's car was all banged up, she said, due to anxiety and the use of her cell phone, while driving. It was very embarrassing to her, but when someone asked her what happened to her car, she just told the truth: She had accidents because she is a nervous, bad driver. They looked at her like, "Huh?" Dad also said she drew attention to herself by driving a car with the bumper hanging and was more likely to be stopped by the police. (Eventually she got it fixed, which was another lesson learned.)

The other day, my mom and dad were fighting loudly, like an airplane flying low, which made me cower, scared me, and hurt my ears. It seemed as if the fight was about money, but I knew better. It was actually about Megan, who had been sick. And they blamed themselves. It made me so nervous that I pulled off another strip of siding.

For a while, my dad wasn't home a lot. Then when he was gone, Mom sat at the table with her coffee, crying and perspiring. (It is good to perspire, I think, but I can't do it myself. Dogs pant.)

Megan thought that my mom was mean to my dad for no reason and thus hated him, and that my dad hated my mom for her hating him and for all the times she was mean to him. This made Mom feel unloved, and Dad already felt unloved, so he went to visit his dad in Kentucky. That in turn made Mom feel sad and emotionally abandoned because whenever he left, it was as if he disappeared into thin air. He stayed a long time, and she couldn't call him because there was bad reception in those hills. In short, he broke her heart. (Later we found out that Dad was actually having a midlife crisis and a nervous breakdown, and nobody noticed.)

Really, it was a misconception, missed communication on all parts. It was a mess. Hate is the opposite of love. But to be apathetic is deadlier, in my opinion. I didn't think we were in a state of apathy yet, so there was still hope.

When my parents married, they had a mission: to have Megan and give her the best in life. They were one. But after Megan grew up, there was more than just an empty nest; there was nothing left. (No other dogs and no grannies were in the picture.) Mom once read (and told me through the airwaves) that they were two individuals who had joined as one. Then they became not two individuals again but one individual cut in half: two halves, each disillusioned and hurting.

When Mom and Dad were in this bad frame of mind, Mom got to thinking that Meg didn't love her anymore either, or that she loved Dad more. This made Meg question whether that was true. There were a lot of hurt souls. Mom said she was going to leave, instead of telling the truth that she was hurting and wanted to run away, which was what Dad was already doing. (Well, I knew that if my mom left for good, I would be right by her side. She proved that when she had left me twice and returned both times. She is my soul mate.)

Megan had been ill, after all, and it must have been hard to watch her be sick—and to watch Dad run away from his feelings and not be there for them. Though Mom was by Meg's side at the hospital, holding her hand and making her laugh, when Meg felt better, it was Mom she was angry with, not Dad. They say a child sticks up for the parent who hurts her more. The child feels unworthy, so she tries harder to be loved by that missing parent. You know what I say? Feel the feeling, then let it go. Face it; otherwise you will eat too much or drink too much, bring an early death on yourself, and lose God for good. But who am I? I'm only a dog who is so young but feels so old.

Megan told Mom that she hated her (she didn't), but the next day, she invited Mom to go with her and a guy friend to the lake. Mom was in a chair with an umbrella, feet down where the water could swoosh over them, feeling old, wondering what the heck she was doing there, allergic to the sun and all, and when only the day before Megan had told her off. But Megan had invited her, and whenever Megan spoke, Mom jumped.

Mom finally got up, dug her feet into the sand, and said that for the moment, they were planted there, with imaginary roots, to Earth and to Mother Nature, which can heal, center, and ground. A speck of recognition appeared in Megan's eyes, realizing a truth that is deep inside us all, but then her hair blew, and in defiance she shook away a strand that had fallen into her face. There was a brief connection to another world. Mom had fed her own soul and Meg's (without Meg knowing, and without even Mom knowing). Then Mom went back to a reality of worry about her kid under *another* sort of umbrella—a dark one—above her.

I'm glad I'm not a mom. Just by the way my mom treats me, a pet, putting me almost first, wanting only the best for me, I can't imagine the anguish she went through with Megan, her kid, not appreciating her at all. Mom's only baby was loosening the ties, pulling, jerking, breaking the ropes of her heart. (Megan wanted to go to a college far, far away in a magical land called California. It's better than Ireland, where some of her classmates were going. Yeah right, maybe for a trip.) The transparent umbilical cord will always be there, but it was hard to decipher that it was there at that raw time.

When Megan felt better, she told the truth: Mom is her emotional haven, Dad is her rock, and she needs them both. What Mom needed to learn is that life can take away your child, but it can't take away the love for your child. (She knew it intellectually, but she needed to feel it.)

To placate herself, Mom got a tattoo with a sun, a moon, and stars above the name Megan. She said she wanted the most beautiful name in the world on her leg forever. When Mom conceived Megan, she felt she knew exactly when Megan's spirit entered her body because there were little stars and lights above her. (Or was it the lights of Las Vegas where she and Dad had honeymooned?) Of course, the tattoo hurt like hell and got infected, and Mom was put on an antibiotic that made her sick. Being sick was better than losing a leg, though. All this for a tattoo that was supposed to take the place of Megan but really wouldn't.

Meg (who, being a teen, knows everything) and Mom once had a talk on spiritual beliefs. Meg slammed Mom for hers, saying she didn't believe a word of what Mom believes (another jab at Mom for breathing). Mom then asked Megan what her beliefs were. Well, Meg said she believed in God, in good and happiness and fun. Mom thought that wasn't bad at all.

You have them only to lose them. You lose them after you raise them.

# Chapter 8

## BOB

Bob is my best friend. I love him. He gives me bones, the real deal and not the grocery store fakes. He loved Domino and Dice. I know he loved Domino the best; I could see it in his eyes, when he talked about him. And, he looked at Dice and told me there was something kind of innocent about him. He now has both of their pictures on the Bible in the back house. He was around when Domino and Dice were babies, and then he came around again, in their twilight years, to bid them farewell. I think. (And to meet me.)

He was with my parents on and off for many years. He had no family. He was kind of different, but we are all different. He slept in the garage at my parents' first house, after staying in the finished basement a while. My parents had done him a favor to take him in, but when he wore out his welcome, they told him he had to get another place. Well, he did. The garage! And when the weather got warmer, instead of leaving the cold garage and getting a nice apartment, he moved into a tent in the back yard; Megan's tent! And my parents couldn't get him out! (After that, they NEVER put up another tent for Megan!! The only other one she had was when she was younger from her Aunt Mellie. They put it on Meg's bed, to let her sleep under, to get her to fall asleep.) In the winter, Bob froze in the garage. Domino and Dice slept inside the warm house, and Bob was freezing in the garage. There's something wrong with that. But what could my family do? He never paid his way, and my parents had given him so many chances. When my parents moved and rented the house out, it took Bob forever to get his stuff out of the garage. Some of it even went on the curb lawn, put out by the renters. So, Mom felt bad about Bob being outside with no heat. But later on, much later on, things have a way of repeating themselves. Mom had the opportunity to turn off his heat yet again one day during one of the coldest winters. This occurred when my parents let him rent another property, the house in the back; the disconnected mother-in-law suite that was once Granny's habitat. My mom then said he was soul family (after Dad's numerous prods to take Bob in) and it was time to make amends. And maybe he learned. Dad thought of course he learned as Dad got the first six months' rent up front. The poet Robert Frost said, "Home is when you have to go there, they have to take you in," from the poem *Death of the Hired Hand*, and it really applies here.

When Bob lived in the back house, he always had something magical in the garage (another garage!) for all of us, for when we needed a lilt in our step. He would give it to us, out of the goodness of his soul. And before we ever bought anything, we asked Bob first as he probably had it. But it's really true, "When it's over, it's over" and our time was about to be over with Bob for good because he wasn't paying his rent again. After a challenge, he would be gone, never to be in my parents' lives, again. Never. "Never say never."

Bob wouldn't be leaving by choice. Or, maybe he was. He didn't seem to be too upset about it. Mom and Megan cried sometimes as he was loading his stuff. But Bob doesn't pay his way. He had moved in and taken over our whole yard, while staying in the back house. And he had all this stuff, err antiques, just like before, which instead of applying himself and selling some of them and paying for his keep, he hoarded them. But when he did sell, he made great money. The motto is, you just can't keep buying without selling some first. But I figured it out. Due to being an orphan, and having a kind but sickly mom adopt him and then die an early death, what else did he have? The garage being full was like a fridge full of food, psychologically representing his mother, his security. He'd sit outside all day long (me often by his side, wagging a slow tail, taking it all in through osmosis) in the summer, washing and polishing his wares with a look of pride, and the peace of mind knowing that, for all his transience, he would never be desolate, or at least in his mind he wouldn't be because as far as I am concerned, he was soon to be destitute. Physically, at least. If only someone could get it across to him that when you empty the fridge, you can buy more food.

Bob was a puzzle. A bunch of pieces that didn't go together. For as confused as he was, he was so organized when it came to his antiques. The garage had stacks and stacks of boxes, each labeled, filed alphabetically with all his stored treasures. It hurt my parents to tell him he had to get out, but they were able to let it go, when they realized, in reality, moving was what he felt the most comfortable doing. Packing and moving from place to place. Staying with friends, treasures intact, until he wears his welcome out, and then having to move again. A wanderer. If he could only learn, to work in the winter, *a real job,* when antiquing was slow, and then seek and *sell* them in the summer. And pay his rent. Something so simple. But that just might be his life-long lesson, and I can't be the judge.

One day, Bob was acting real strange. Harmless as his thoughts were, they often got the best of him when he did this gyration in his mind, worrying about all the gossip, he was gossiping about.

He wanted to have a talk with me and Mom. Our heads were spinning, listening to him. Something about Angie ** divorce ** Mark ** Scorpio ** Don **jail ** crook ** he'll have all your land before it's all over ** Lottie ** an Aries ** woe ** jealous ** Lori Drew ** Nicole ** my dad ** or whatever, something like that. Phew. My head started to hurt, I had to sign out. I always try to put some fun in the dys*function*, but this was just too much. I scratched on the door and had to go in, even before Mom.

When he finally moved, for a while I would jump up on the back fence, waiting for him to give me another goody until my heart caught up with my brain that his house was now empty.

Glory be! The all good must have intervened at least for the moment because he was still here. He must have paid some rent. He was still cleaning the garage, fire hazard that it was. He was helping my mom with the weeds, the house, and I suppose this is how it is going to be, until the next time, when a misunderstanding provokes the thought that it was time for him to start packing again.

Until then I will enjoy the smell of Murphy's Oil Soap, as Bob polishes.

I guess "It's not over 'til it's over." Yogi Berra said that. And for that moment, the game wasn't over for Bob. But trust me, it would be soon.

# Chapter 9

## LILAH

Lilah was an example of a puppy born into the world defective due to irresponsible breeding practices. Her back legs were not strong due to undeveloped muscles or, worse yet, maybe fraught with neurological problems because of early inadequate nutrition. Her slightly larger head had the sweetest face and biggest eyes, and it could not be supported by her little neck. She was a purebred Jack Russell terrier but not "perfect," so she was thrown away, infested with fleas and ticks, left to die in a barn with the horses. Right from the start, she could have been rescued (who would want her?) by someone with a big heart (you guessed it—Mom!) or "put to sleep," which probably would have been the most humane of all the choices. She was a runt and a preemie, and her mother had died in childbirth. Could she have had it any worse? She was minuscule in size but not in heart, and another example of an unwanted dog, a burden to society, no matter how small she was. She would tax society in some way, then she would end up an ash in the dirt.

I related to Lilah's story because I was born defective and unwanted, too. I was almost thrown away, too, in this throwaway society. Even with all my problems, I deserved to live as did Lilah because someone messed around and made us so. Looking at her really moved me. When I met her, I just lay back and didn't pounce, even though I felt so much joy that she was here and maybe would want to play soon.

I might have known something was up that summer day in July. Mom brought me the biggest bone ever, kissed me all day long, sang, and whistled with all the faith in the world because my dad was coming home from the hills with a gift for her. (The previous time, he had brought her a Bunn coffeemaker.) He had gone

yet again to visit his father in Kentucky. Well, that day he was coming home, and Mom trusted, like a child on Christmas (just how she was when she first met me).

Dad and his brother drove up, and my mom and Meg ran outside, all happy-go-lucky, and brought in a box. What contraption was inside? Something fuzzy? No. Maybe a Kong with legs? No.

Maybe a critter or a rodent? *No.* A dog. A *dog?* A friend for me? Good humans all around, but I was still so glad to see something furry coming over the threshold, the prettiest angel in the world. The dog looked as if it were their gift, but I was the true recipient.

I now present you with Delilah Dulcinae Mullins! Lilah for short. I was so happy! Hubba, hubba. A little delight, with an angelic middle name. It was the name of the fair maiden of *Man of La Mancha*, "The Impossible Dream" musical, shortened by Dad from Dulcinea to Dulcinae. (Here we go again, Mom and her plays.) "To dream the impossible dream. . . ." With a name like that, what could go wrong?

No matter how tiny Lilah was, we would bridge the gap, and she would become my forever friend. I was here to show her the way. That is why I really stayed in the background as she was being groomed for me, being made stronger to be ready for my big paws. But that didn't stop me from adoring glances because she was adorable.

This time my dad was Father Teresa. He saved her, like my mom saved me. Of all the healthy puppies there, he picked the little sad one, the lowly one, for Mom, and she opened her arms wide for Lilah, as always.

The little gal loved to eat. "Eh, eh, eh," she squeaked when food was around. I think the goose liver endeared us to her, forever. She licked her lips when she was thirsty. She was so smart. She would whine for a minute, and Mom and Meg would put her on a potty pad, where she immediately did what she was supposed to do. But later on, "the experts" said that was just a pure instinct to survive. Hmm, what do they know?

My mom had visions of a happy girl, maybe not the sharpest animal but getting around with a harness and wheels in the back. We had had her for ten days, and she was out of the woods, except for those legs.

It was Friday and Mom and Megan had just fed her a bottle of puppy milk, which she loved. Her belly was full and content, and she made a quiet noise that sounded like a purr.

*But now she's with her four-legged mama.*

Another surprise! Lilah died.

RIP, Delilah Dulcinae Mullins.

She was up in heaven now, but one good thing about her brief time with us was that she had brought out Megan's ability to love.

# Chapter 10

## I Z Z I E

The same night Lilah died, Mom and Megan were in a panic. Megan was devastated. Lilah was really *her* baby. Her first, ever, that she herself had taken responsibility for, cared for, and loved. As I said, Delilah opened Megan's heart.

Mom and Meg got this brainy idea to ease the pain. They looked in the paper for another dog, and they found one. So they brought me in the car with them, *for solidarity,* to bond more with me, to thank God they still had me. We went to Aurora, about an hour away, to check out a five-month-old Jack Russell terrier who was being sold for $150. Wow, this was to be *it.* Megan said that if she liked the terrier, it would be hers. But Mom said no, they had to agree. Mom was driving a bit fast, getting lost in the dark, asking for directions on the phone, making wrong turns. She entered the interstate at the truck entrance, oh my.

Well, we finally got there, and apparently the dog was not what they wanted *at all*. So one minute in the door, one minute out the door—it had taken us longer to get there. They thanked the lady and pointed to me—running back and forth in the car, an anxiety attack overtaking me, nose marks all over the windows. They said their pup was too hyper, and honestly, one hyper one was enough. What a disappointment. Such sobs were heard on the way home, my whining not the only sound. This just made the hurt worse.

Mom made a joke about putting another dog in the cage before Dad came home from yet another trip. He wouldn't know the difference, being blind and all. She was kidding, of course, but Meg expanded on that idea and said she just wanted to look at the pet store puppies. The place had Mom and Meg put on gowns and plastic gloves to hold the puppies; it seemed top notch. We came to find out later, though, that Mom and Meg were helping to support and foster puppy mills because that is precisely where our new dog came from. Well, don't love the action but love the dog, or something like that.

There we had it. So Delilah was gone, the Aurora deal was off, and like a revolving door, enter Izabella Katarina—the middle name came from the great Olympic ice skating star Katarina Witt. Dad gave her that middle name because he had always liked it as he liked the star, and Izzie looked like a cat.

Now this one rocked my Gibraltar. What the heck were these people doing, bringing in all these dogs? Mom always says that if you look for trouble long enough, you'll find it. One mistake doesn't warrant two, but this family seemed to like that sort of thing. One day after Delilah's death, the gnat was in her cage. This time, forget bringing me a friend. I felt sick, I felt as if I wasn't enough for them. I got this horrible feeling in the pit of my stomach that I wasn't wanted anymore. Sometimes I feel self-conscious about my spots, but this one had more problems than I did.

She had ears that looked as if they came straight out of the Mickey Mouse Club and were ready to take off any minute. She reminded me of one of those uppity ladies at the opera, looking all around and holding her glasses up to her eyes. To put it bluntly, she was a snob, and I did not like her one bit. Life would never be the same; I had more seniority, but she became my new boss in life.

When she first arrived, she ran around the house like a maniac. It made you dizzy. Nobody could catch her. My brain and reflexes needed a minute to adjust, so I could run, too. She didn't listen, just like me, but she could hear. She did you-know-what in her cage all the time. She was doing it *a lot*. The one time I looked, she had a cigar sticking out of her mouth. Well, it wasn't a cigar, if you know what I mean. She was a poo-poo girl, not a foo-foo. She piddled in her cage, which was meant for kitchen floors, not dog dens.

She became housebroken, but she often did her business in *my* bed, so we had to keep *my* cage door locked when I wasn't in it. You know, sometimes it would have been nice to go in and out when I felt like it, but no, not with this one. And so, so little she was, but when she did happen to get in, I couldn't get her out. Somehow that still perplexes me.

Izzie's parents were abused and being used to breed puppy litter after another. Izzie was healthy, but then she started holding her leg funny. It turned out she needed a $1,500 surgery because she had Legg-Calvé-Perthes Disease. It was like a hip replacement when she was only a couple months old. Poor baby. The vet said he was sure that both of her parents carried the gene for the disease, so just think of all the Izzies who are out there with this disease.

When her leg was messed up, she hardly barked, or ran around like a fool anymore. Doc said she was a brave puppy because it was a painful thing to have. This all reinforced the idea of Mom *never*

getting another dog from a breeder (or at least an inexperienced one); she would always rescue one instead.

I got agitated with Izzie's shrill bark, which came almost *right after* she got her leg fixed. Even I could hear it. Whine, whine, whine, this foxy terrier. Oh brother. I mean oh sister. She was a girl, right? Yep.

Mom paid attention to me, but it wasn't the same, so I was a little off-center. Mom and I were always a team. But alas, maybe this one, too, was a potential friend for me. I doubted it. She sure was a cocky thing.

# Chapter 11

### RUNNING

Life wasn't too good after Izzie arrived. Those planes were flying low again.

Mom sure had her emotional ups and downs. She had such a hard road sometimes. I felt so sorry for her, and because I am an emotional sieve, I rode the bumps with her.

One day Mom left again. She looked upset. All I could do the whole time she was gone was bite my nails—bite, spew the nail out. I wondered what would happen with Izzie and me if she didn't return, and with Megan, who needed her so. (Meg was still sick off and on, but with something a doctor couldn't mend. It was called growing up.) And Dad! It wasn't that she was trying to prove something; she often just had this need to run away. Don't we all?

Sometimes, winter or not, I want to just go to the doggie park and run and run and run.

I wondered how my book would end. Then after she came back, I saw it wouldn't end until I was dead! Amen! I was so glad she was home again. There were miles of smiles from me. Err, smarls. (A Dalmatian smile that is really a snarl = smarl.)

Most of the time, Mom was there 101 percent, always keeping the faith. She wrote the bills. Did her best to keep the house nice. Shopped for groceries. Drove the whole family around. Took me to the vet. Washed clothes and dishes. Cooked. Cleaned. Helped with Meg's engineering homework. *Engineering homework?!* Well, she'd pick out an answer that was wrong, and then Meg would say, "Give it here, and I'll show you the correct answer." Harrumph.

Megan had good study skills because when she was in grade school, Mom helped her with her homework every evening after supper. That was their ritual. Oh, and Mom tutored her to death. Megan asked Mom one day how much longer did she have to go through this; Mom said it would be when she started applying herself, which she did the very next day. That was before my time, and thank goodness Mom got it out of her system because there was a training manual for me, and she wasn't as strict with me as she was with Megan.

Mom lives in pain a lot of the time. I can smell it on her. And work, as in employment, was cut short for her. Thus, her only request was that when she died, her headstone would read: "When I felt good, I worked hard." Little did she know that someday she would work again, and it would be a wonderful job. All I know is that an eclipse must have happened that night she left and came back, and Jupiter must have been with us all because she returned to the home fires, to literally put out the flames. (Actual pan flames. Courtesy of Dexter?)

When Granny was dying, that is just what she said to Mom: "Go home and put out your smoke." Later she said, "Where is your family?" (It was coming apart at the seams.) "I need to see them as it's almost the end of the story." And it was. How prophetic.

Izzie and I started to bond. Her ears started to relax, and she eventually grew into them. No smiles or flinches of the face, but there were those expressive ears. Actually, I take that back: Her whole face would soften at times, which made her look adoringly at you, and that took the place of a smile.

She seemed to be reflective. I was finally beginning to see her point of view. How would you like it if everything was enormously bigger than you? No wonder she seemed a bit neurotic. Who cares, though? I was the ultimate neurotic. (Or Mom was, ha ha.)

I want you to ponder this: If you see a truck on the road, do you see just the truck or the guy inside driving the truck? I think you just see the truck. To Izzie, we were all trucks, and she didn't really see what was inside. She had to make sure that we weren't going to run her over (especially blind dads), that we were loving people, God inside us, driving the truck of life, and that love has no age or weight.

# Chapter 12

## MOO-MOO

Moo-Moo the Min-Pin (a Miniature Pinscher, in case you're wondering) is my cousin and a little snoot, but my mom loves him—or at least she did. He is black, sleek, and good looking. For a treat, he jumps up and does a dance, smiles, claps, and prays, and when he howls it sounds like "I love you" and "I wanna go." What a little show-off.

He can be a loaded gun at times and bite. Everybody ignores that, though. He could use a bit of Prozac, too, if I say so. All this was because he was abused before. Then Mom's in-laws saw him walking down a dirt road and kids throwing rocks at him, so they put him in their car and took him home. They have two other Min-Pins, plus other breeds, that all found them, not the other way around. This happened with their first dog, Trixie, who found them. Trixie smiled, too. Now there is the dancing Bear, who used to plop on your head, and Candace and Fred, *huh?* Oh, and Geezer. A crew of entertainment, all rolled in one. Well, I'm twice the dog (maybe three times) that Moo-Moo or any of them are.

Methinks someone is a bit jealous.

Well, Moo-Moo dug his teeth into Megan's leg recently, resulting in a pretty severe cut. Good thing she had her jeans on. He bit her, and Mom's not too eager to call him her boy anymore.

# Chapter 13

## THE STORM

It was so dry and humid, actually hot. I could see the steam rising from the concrete. It hurt my feet, not to mention I was not myself that day or hadn't been for a whole week, but no one had noticed. Mom didn't leave me outside for long. She never did, if there was any bit of danger, like a mean sun. Mom took care of me better than Mother Dog, and my dad seemed to love me more every day (even if I had chewed the TV wires again). Dad said it was unusual to have it so windy without any rain. It was like a dust storm.

Inside everyone was watching cable, talking about the pending Hurricane Ike, soon to hit Texas. It would not touch us, but we were feeling a bit of it, evident in the unusual weather we were experiencing. Mom said we were lucky because we lived in God's country, and we were not to ever take advantage of that thought but instead remain humble because nobody really knew when tragedy would befall them next.

I had had this pain for about a week. I would throw up my food, and Mom kept an eye on me, but Dad, true to his nature, said it was just puppy stuff because we eat everything. Yes, at all 90 pounds of me (at that time), I was still considered a pup. But that day, the pain was worse. I couldn't even lift my leg, and when I squatted, for as hard as I tried, not too much came out of me. Sometimes the urine would just leak from me. I had lived with this pain for what seemed like forever, so what did that mean? It was brewing, just like the weather, I guess, getting hotter and hotter. Megan noticed me then, trying to squat in the house. She saw the little puddles. I saw her tell Mom. I was in a daze. No, actually, I was delirious.

On the couch, hurting so much, all eyes peeled to the screen, suddenly the wind kicked up as the power went out, and I went out next, and it was the end.

*The End?*

(What transpires next is either a dream, a past life experience, or a case where I went to the light and came back. You decide.)

Yes, the end, and the end of the book. Sigh. (I saw the fear in their eyes, and the surprise that I had died.) Addressing all the breeders in the world, Mom wrote in the epilogue that she would never say to put a deaf dog to sleep, but with all the problems I had, everyone should be warned what a challenge it could be, and how sad, and with that information, they should make an intelligent, loving decision. They should make sure that they know what they are doing and that they should be careful with overbreeding. That a dog should be created for the love of the breed, not for money. How they adopted me, only for this ultimate blow.

*Dead.*

Place: Adriatic Coast, Dalmatia, Croatia

It was a gorgeous, sunlit day. I looked all around for my family. Was I in heaven? Did we not all come together? What a shame. It was like a dream. I saw Getta and Rok, and their parents, Anastasia and Franusch.

"Tockica (pronounced Tojka), Tockica!" They called me, and I came as I was well behaved. (Tockica? Yet another name, sigh. It's a Croatian word that means "spot.")

They were poor but happy because they always had enough. A special joy came to them not in material ways, but from the beauty of the land that they worked and tilled. The few palm trees flourished in the subtropical climate. I saw beautiful purple irises, the flower of Croatia. I don't know if they were wild when the settlers first came or if a Dalmatian (yes, a person from Dalmatia, Croatia, is also a Dalmatian) planted them. Most everyone grew figs, pumpkins, and watermelons in their gardens. The Adriatic Sea was as blue as the sky. It was so clear that you could see the fish, and it was so clean that you could swim next to them when you weren't fishing.

Once a week Anastasia went to the market to buy a soup bone that made enough for a big, hearty stew. Franusch, who was strong and hardworking, was grateful for what was put on the table before him. On the days it was a beef bone, they often gave me a treat! (Smarl!)

I was upset that I couldn't find my family. I loved them so much. (Are you my family?) When they weren't there, I thought I'd rather be together with them than alone in heaven. Getta and Rok were jumping and playing as they always did. Anastasia was hanging out the wash. I sat on the terrain, with its different colored rocks and grass peeking out, shining like emeralds from the morning dew. It was so peaceful and looked like a painting. But then the sun went down, gray was all around, and playtime was halted due to a big storm that came out of nowhere, that barely let them retrieve their toys and get safely in the house. Their mom and dad attempted to gather the rest of their belongings when a torrential rain and howling wind came and gathered them and the children. "Tockica!" I heard my name, and it took me next.

Then, instead of resting a bit and doing my life review, I grabbed a head with no ears. I would be too big. I would have two different eyes, a brown one and a blue one, wild like a wolf. I would have extra baggage. Then it was time. There came a sloshing forth warm, muddy waters rushing in, me storming out the broken drain, silence all around again.

I awoke to my mom's worried face. Mama Victoria. This life. Fading in and out, I saw she was calling a vet *with* power (as it was out all over) and heading out because this was an emergency. My father gathered me up and took me in. It turned out that I had a stone and an infection. They caught it just in time, before the urine backed up the other way and poisoned me. A tube was put up me to flush out the stone while my dad held me as I moaned on the table. The tube had to go up twice, and it hurt so much. A shot to calm me. Then a catheter, so a stone would not get blocked again, until they knew what was going on. My urine was leaking. They took some of it, then my blood and an X-ray, which all determined I was safe. My life was saved. At last my family was here, *this family*, and we would go home.

I now had a new affliction. I was a Dalmatian with too many alkali crystals in my urine that formed stones. Gone for always were the milk bones and rawhide treats, the table scraps. I was left only with a prescription food that cost a fortune and tasted like sh_t but was very fattening and rich.

Speaking of past lives: I figured out that Izzie was named Toya in that life. She missed the storm. Tockica and Toya, brother and sister from the same litter, in a different life. That's why she thinks she's so big.

Tragedies like this usually made you stronger, and often out of extreme bad came profound good. Character was built. That was true for me. (Must have been that grand trine I was born with in my astrological chart!) From that day on, Dad let me sleep in their bed, and all around, I felt more secure. If I was put outside for a while or in my cage when they left, it was okay because I looked at it like my alone time—a time for reverie, a time to ponder more book ideas, rather than a time for the crippling fear that used to overtake me. Maybe that was my job in life: to sometimes be in my cage.

Also, Megan had been walking me—through the grass! I would roll around and wallow, soaking up all the green. Oh, life was so verdant!

Well, for a couple of nights, we were fine with the sleeping arrangements. But one night, Izzie got up and did her business, right on the pastel sheets. I thought, *Well, I could beat that.* So I did my thing. Mom woke up, saw what Izzie did. Ew, bad. Stripped the bed. I got that look on my face, and she knew right away that Izzie wasn't the only culprit. Did I really do that? Or was it guilt by association? Geesh, I didn't know. Mom still wonders how we got away with it and how they stayed asleep with all the commotion. We were both kicked out of their bed. Oh well; kids (err, dogs), at least grown-up ones, aren't supposed to sleep with their parents, anyway.

I certainly must have had my redeeming qualities because within two days, I was back in their bed. Izzie wasn't allowed because (a) she was incontinent (b) she bit, and that's not right. But then she was in Megan's bed, being bad.

I couldn't analyze this too much because it was night, and my brain was tired.

# Chapter 14

## IZZIE'S DREAM

Izzie visited Granny a couple times at the nursing home, and she had a ball. She made many friends there, many different "aunts" and "uncles." One man, though—who always yelled, "Help me, help me!"—saw her and screamed, "Get that dog out of here [all four pounds of her]! She's gonna *bleep* all over the place!"

One day after Izzie was there, Granny came down with something very contagious. Mom was upset, hoping that Izzie hadn't caught it. Life was, after all, hard enough. Whenever Granny got sick, Mom would panic and think it was the end. Granny had many close calls but always pulled out of it, not ready to leave the planet yet. Mom didn't know what she would do when that fateful day came. I didn't know either.

Mom always said she shared a heart with Granny, so in preparation for the ultimate end, Mom, in a meditative state, began to give Granny back the part of the heart that belonged to her. Mom took her own part back, too, putting the pieces back in their respective places, where they belonged. Then each had her own *whole* heart back again. Mom and Granny had had lessons so big in this life— too much for one person to handle—so they had decided to share a heart this time around. Each was now as it should be: intact.

An egg separates and divides to make two wholes or more. Identical twins share a sac, and no matter how far they find themselves from each other, what one does, the other does, too, in some way. They are two for the price of one. Well, Granny and Mom were not twins or twin souls. They were just always in each other's pockets because they shared a heart. Simple as that. (Why Mom didn't have a bed right next to Granny at the home was beyond me.) No more would there be that feeling of a brick pressing on Mom's chest, making it difficult to breathe when she went to bed and when she thought of Granny dying, because all was indeed right with the night. At least that night.

I knew Granny better than anyone, even though I was there only once to see her. (And from that day on, Granny always asked about me, the funky Dalmatian who didn't have his head on straight, who always made her laugh when Mom told my stories.) I knew her through my mom's energy, for I am a psychic dog. But Izzie had this dream about her, and in a way it was eerie and prophetic and puzzling, how she knew so much about Granny, having gone there only a couple of times.

*Granny was driving a big, white Cadillac to paradise. She always felt as if she were going to heaven when she was on her way to play bingo. There were a couple of clouds in her way, blocking the sun. Granny tooted and said, "Jackass." The bingo hall was all lit up. It had gold bingo chips and pure stainless steel "arms" on the slot machines. She was always lucky, and as usual, she won. She got new, crisp money that was verdant, like Uncle Dex's grass that he often wallowed in. After that, she went to church. When Mass was finished, she saw that a funeral was about to start. She knew the family, so she paid her respects. She told the family that she hadn't known of their loss because she hadn't read the obituaries in a couple of days. Then Granny went to the church basement with her friends Lena and Helen for donuts. When she walked into the room, a big crowd yelled, "Surprise!" Then came the most wonderful party. A lot of relatives she hadn't seen in a while were there. Granny was shy but looked downright rude as she started scratching her scratch-offs, a gift from Aunt Katherine. (Maybe it was pathetic, because in some respects Granny was the social butterfly, but in other instances, she was socially inept.) Her husband, Gus, was late and there in his work clothes. He just wanted to stop in for a minute. He didn't like parties. Aunt Mellie was holding Gracie, who was yelling "Cookie, cookie!" that she wanted from Granny, also known as the cookie lady. After the party was over, Granny was tired and went to lie down for a much needed rest. When she awoke, like a bird she went to her new spot: to be perched on Vickie's shoulder forever. One of the most beautiful birds in the entire world and in the Animal Kingdom of Heaven: the black crow.*

Granny was sick again, and this time she was asking questions like this: "Should I hand out my candy bars in case I die?" My mom helped her get in bed every night as she grew weaker and weaker.

One day that day will come, and down will come the falls, and Mom will drown in it all.

# Chapter 15

## A HOUSE

The bricks were crumbling. The driveway was cracked into slabs.
Part of the siding was off, thanks to a dog named Dexter (hunkered
down, sorry). Many windows on the sun porch had fallen out. The
carpet on the porch was damp (and faded) from the rain/snow
getting through the missing windows. Holes were in the screens.
The blinds all over the house wouldn't close, especially the ones on
the front picture window. The paint on the walls was old, chipping,
and full of dog scratches on the white bedroom doors (hunkering
again), and the wallpaper was peeling in certain rooms. The garage
and the back house needed new roofs. The basement was wet, with
black mold all over it. There was no money to fix this—no money
at all. Everything was breaking down, waiting to fall in a river
of tears.

That's what you call a broken home.

Apple core sitting in the center of a banana peel, sprinkled with grape seeds. Orange and grapefruit rinds arranged all around, with peach stones and a cup of hot tea, half empty.

My mom was just one person. My dad was hanging out with the prisoners from the jail where he worked. Megan said she was going to Florida. Only Izzie and me would be left. With my luck, we would be separated, and no one would be left except me, or I would be booted out. To this I ask, "What happens when a book ends before its end?"

# Chapter 16

## BINH

Binh came into our family's life when it seemed as if everything was coming to an end. Well, it was, and he helped fill the gap for a while, by uplifting all our spirits. Mom looked at him as if he were her long-lost son. Then she thought he would make a nice son-in-law. Then I think she actually forgot her age when she put on her slightly high heels (rather than her New Balances, which she wore all the time except to bed), and she shook her head like a schoolgirl every time Binh was around. (In short, she made a fool of herself.) That was the summer she put red in her hair. Poor Mom. Poor Dad!

My brothers loved and accepted Binh immediately. Sometimes Dice would sleep by him if he stayed the night. Domino, who had trouble with guests, parked himself right on his feet. When I came into the picture, Binh thought we were all crazy. He didn't like me.

Why, the two older dogs were sick, we had our hands full with all this stress, and he just didn't appreciate my bounciness in jumping from lap to lap. When he spent the night on the couch, he didn't care for my early morning barks, before anybody was up. Whenever he got mad at me, he would *pick me up* and put me in my cage. I didn't like *him,* either.

Binh was of small stature, but you'd never know it because he was strong enough to lift all eighty pounds of me. The strength came from resolve. He was ambidextrous. Once I saw him jump onto the top of a car straight from the ground, just jumping up with the strength of those legs. Nothing got past him.

Binh liked Megan, of course. But Megan was so immature for her age and only liked him as a friend. Or it could have been a fling without the fling, if you know what I mean. (Maybe that pertained to Mom.) In any case, I do think that a monumental relationship occurred. Megan and Binh learned how to be comfortable with the opposite sex, enjoying each other's company as friends often do before they get into a relationship (yes, it happens). It was a big learning experience for both of them. They both learned about companionship.

Binh was always spoiling Megan, and he had good taste as Megan did, so she graciously accepted his presents, all wide-eyed like the eighteen-year-old kid/woman she was when they first met. But he was older by seven years—too old for her, actually—and she could never reciprocate or totally accept him in the way he wanted to be accepted. He had been in a relationship before he came into our picture, but he never talked about it. With Megan, though, he did all the giving, and he was ready. Megan learned how to take from a young man, and Binh learned how to give. Maybe the next time,

Binh would get the whole package, a relationship of give and take as it should be. Megan needed to learn how to give, be knocked off her feet, feel what it was like to love, have her heart go kerplunk. Then she, too, would be close to the real thing.

Mom had a dream that Binh went to culinary school. It was a long-lost goal of his that was stepped on because of fear and other responsibilities. Under the direction of my family, he actually signed up to go. I'm not saying my mom's hocus-pocus powers cajoled him to do this. It was his destiny to go, and we happened to be in his life, to give a little nudge when it all finally came together for him. He went and worked on becoming the best chef in the world, traveling all over Europe for his internship, and then he planned on staying in one place, wherever he found a job.

Needless to say, the friendship of three years ended abruptly. I think Binh loved her, but feelings weren't the same, so he had the sense to get out. Ouch. But hopefully he was a better person than he had been before.

Megan was apathetic (did something bad happen between them?) and Dad didn't seem to think anything was wrong. But I think my mom never got over him not being her son or future son-in-law, or maybe she was sad that she hadn't met Binh under different circumstances, at another place and time.

He didn't call or answer our calls.

But then eventually he did. His wounds healed. Friends again.

# Chapter 17

## A LESSON IN BUDGETING

If you know that a lot needs to be fixed, but you don't know where to begin, just start fixing anything that needs it. When there are lots of questions but you don't know the answers, just keep asking questions. Question me an answer: That became Mom's new mantra. Every time she got into the car, she started asking herself, due to high gas costs, *Is this trip really necessary?* Did she compare prices of gas at different stations when she was out and about? When she bought something, did she really need it? Was it necessary to get expensive haircuts and manicures? Did she need to talk so much on the cell phone? Did the family need to eat out so much at fast-food places and restaurants? She made a meal every day, whether the family ate it or not, and if they still chose to eat out, she had no part of it. When you drive the getaway car, you, too, are at fault; you're considered to be doing wrong, too.

Did she absolutely need to go to the doctor? Did Izzie and I need vet care by a doc who was halfway across town because he was "the best" but much more expensive? Cripes, we're dogs, for goodness sake. Did we have to go out so much? Maybe it was time to stop running for every little thing. Did we need to get our prescriptions at the drugstore, or could we order them by mail, which was cheaper? Now that was a deal, a three-month supply for the price of two months. Did the air conditioner have to be on all the time? Let in some fresh air sometimes. Did the heat have to be so warm on a blustery day? That's why sweaters were invented.

Unplug those appliances! Turn off the lights when you leave the room and turn off the radios and TVs when you're not watching them. Shut the doors.

There you have it. Maybe things (anything) would get better if Mom followed her new set of rules.

# Chapter 18

## GRANNY'S DECLINE

Mom went to see Granny one day; her dress was on backward, the lights were off, and she was asleep and wheezing. She was sleeping like a baby, so Mom didn't disturb her. Mom called later to see if Granny was eating supper, and Granny said yes, but when Mom asked what, Granny said she didn't know. I think it was fair to say that Granny was slipping further. Mom asked Dad if he ever thought of visiting her; she wondered whether maybe Granny wanted to die but wouldn't until he came to visit her. He said he would go the next day, but tomorrow never comes.

The cousins from Elyria came to see her, and Granny smiled sweetly like a baby. She wasn't her usual blunt self, telling her visitors to leave when she was tired. She would lie down, take a little snooze, then get up and talk some more. Happiness was all around.

Granny started saying things like this: "Vickie said I am going to hell." She was looking for Mom's phone number in the newspaper, telling us that the nurses on the floor were asking for her obituary.

One nurse said, "Margaret, if you don't eat, you will die."

She answered, "Goodbye!" So typical of Granny's humor.

What a year it was turning out to be. Mom cared for and lost her dogs. She thought she would probably lose her mom, daughter, and husband all at once. Her mind, too. But hopefully not her dog.

It was the first Christmas with no presents under the tree and not a lot of food in the house. It was Megan's last year at home before college. In previous years, the presents were stacked up almost to the ceiling. But this year, with Mom and Dad not getting along and not working together, and the money so tight, there was nothing. (Actually Binh and his mom got together and made sure Meg had a real nice Christmas.) Wow, there were some wounds here that were going to need some healing. There had to be another way to balance the yin and the yang. Maybe, next year, just a few presents under the tree?

Mom, in a reflective mood, took down the tree ornaments. She told me that you can really tell the type of person you are by how you decorate a tree. Someone who puts the tree in a corner, with all the lights and bulbs just in the front of the tree, is someone who is hiding something.

# Chapter 19

## SICK

Mom, Dad, and Megan all had bad colds. The same cold. One of the worst colds. They all kept giving it to each other and catching it from each other. They were trying to keep the towels separate. I knew I should be bringing them warm soup and tissues, medicine, the thermometer, etc., but I'm only a dog, so I just sat there looking at them, allowing them to cough it out all over themselves.

Some would say what tough luck that is, that they are all sick at once, but I call it a type of bonding in a family that hadn't been able to bond for a while. Now when Meg—all nineteen years of her—was scared for a minute, she crawled into bed with my parents. That looked weird, but don't let the psychologists upset you. This, too, was a form of closeness in a family not feeling close anymore. All in all, you have to start somewhere, so how about the bottom?

My mom said that being sick is the next best thing to doing nothing. (No, that's fishing.) When you get sick, your body is telling you that it is tired and needs a rest. So you relax without guilt, and before you know it, you're better. Why not take the time off *before* you get sick?

# Chapter 20

## THE TRIP

It was a Friday morning in December. It started like any other day. Mom let me out, gave me a treat and my pills, let me eat, and then directed me back into the cage for my two hours. Well, when I woke up, I saw that everyone was home, and there was a lot of commotion. What were they up to now? It was always something.

I got past the gate, ran upstairs like I always did but wasn't supposed to, and saw that Izzie's cage was missing. They had probably realized how annoying she was and had gotten rid of her. But that was so not like them. They *save* in this house, not send away. I decided to enjoy it anyway; now they could put their full attention on me. I danced around and whirled my bone up, wanting someone to play, and then it hit me. This was a hollow victory.

Remember how happy I had been when they brought home the first fuzz for me? (Delilah, God bless.) Well, I had just started to like Izzie. Then I realized that you should be careful what you wish for because it just may happen. Izzie was gone. My hair was standing up, the way a cat's does in panic mode, before a big hiss. I leaned against the wall, neutral ground, rather than against my mom. *What if I was next? What if they got rid of me?* The rest is kind of a blur.

They took me to a vet, a different vet at that. (We changed vets a lot because a lot of them did not know what to do with me.) She looked me over and put this nasal stuff up my nose, and then my family left. I went into a big cage with a towel from home, a couple of bones I didn't even like, and a place to run. They treated me like a dog. There were other abandoned animals there, too. But this was so unlike my family to do this to me. I didn't like it one bit. I lay there for days, so sad that my family was gone. I was beyond tears.

(You know what else? My family took me there one more time, and when they heard that all I did was cry, they never took me back there again. I then got to go to a real place, sort of like a spa for dogs, and Izzie got to go with me.)

Later on, Izzie told me that they had taken her to Aunt Bev's, whoever that was. She was a pretty lady with a pretty house. But Bev's dog, Rusty, (a weiner dog) ignored her the whole time. He was cute, but I took it that Rusty wasn't expecting a good look like Izz. She said they were good to her, but she was glad to be home. She said that at first, she couldn't even look at our family because she was mad at them for leaving her at some strange dog's house. She felt even worse when she came home and I wasn't there.

But of course my family came back for me. I might have known. I should learn to trust. I need to learn self-confidence, self-worth. Then I could have made the best of the situation. You can't live in fear. (But they could have told both Izzie and me what was going on.) When they returned, I realized that their departure had nothing to do with hurting Izzie or me, and it couldn't have been that they were fighting because when they came and got me, they were smiling. I hadn't eaten, and Mom said they could hear my barks right through the vet's brick building. It was so good to be home, and Izzie was there, too! We wrestled and played a bit. I found out later that they had gone to Chicago to look at a college with Megan. (Megan just was not gonna quit until she found a way to leave home.) What I didn't understand was why they didn't take Izzie or me. I got on my favorite kitchen chair to ponder all of this a bit and then did something I never did before. I climbed on top of the table.

There began the wheels of change. Binh was back. Mom and Dad, Meg and Binh were looking at things differently. It is as if they had all grown up—until Binh started that romantic stuff again. He went a little bit too far this time, and now he and Megan were friends for never! Period. End of chapter.

# Chapter 21

## FULL CIRCLE

If there is such a thing as Karma, it is a force that initially draws beings together and the bond that is severed if a lesson is learned. If the lesson is learned, and you still stay together, you generate more Karma, or Life Force. Nowadays, Karma doesn't have to last for a whole lifetime or be from a past life; it can be from yesterday. With Earth evolving and the vibrations changing to the higher realms, (retribution) is accomplished, quicker and quicker.

Mom gets "messages" from dreams, especially from her family who are with her but in the spirit world. Those dreams help Mom with her life, as do the empaths and intuitives she often talks to. Those words have a negative connotation in today's society, though maybe they are becoming a little more accepted. Mom associates with ones who are highly educated, evolved beings.

Mom is also pretty psychic herself. When Mom doesn't understand something about me, she often thinks about (or calls) the animal communicator (the dog whisperer) who said the reason I have so many problems, and why I am so sensitive to energy, is because my other family left me tied outside during a bad storm, and I died. When I reached the other side, I couldn't find my family, so I didn't even rest for a minute to do my life review but reincarnated immediately back here in a body that wasn't ready to come back to the earth.

Megan once said that if what the communicator said was true, she was hurt that she, Dad, and Mom weren't the only family I loved. She said that I loved my other family, so maybe she, Mom, and Dad should have just let me die, so I could finally find and be with them. But Mom explained to Megan that those people weren't there, that *they* are my family now, in this life, and that they are here to help me live out my karma, which was cut short in my last life.

Not only was this reading from the communicator important, but there was also something very familiar about it. A dog being outside during a storm and dying. If nothing else, it made Mom feel more compassion for me, the deaf guy locked in his silent world. The one who had such erratic behavior that nobody would want because I was so crazy. The dog she would never part from, no matter what. (I hoped.)

Shh, for a minute. Mom was about to find the key to the riddle, which would dissolve the karma between us. I was going to learn where I came from, where I was going, and why I was here. It would be a coming of age in which I would then know self-love and self-reliance, and sort of like the character Pinocchio, I would become a real boy. Err, dog.

Many years ago, Mom made a trip to Maui, Hawaii, to visit her cousin Angela. It was so unlike Mom to travel to such a faraway place as she was afraid of flying *and* water. But somehow fate took her there, all day on a plane over the Pacific Ocean, to a place intoxicatingly beautiful, with the beauty and smell of flowers, and serenity all around. Well, the night before she was to come home, there came a horrible storm that kept her up all night. It felt like a bad omen. Torrents of rain beating on the roof and the pavement. All the splendor of the place, a place with almost too much beauty, now soaked, muddy all over.

The howling of the wind came with a different howl: the mournful barks of a dog in dismay, tied outside while it was pouring, rain soaking him, hail hitting him, and wind blowing him all around. Mom was horrified and brokenhearted that someone would be so thoughtless as to let that happen to one of God's creatures. She immediately told her cousin to *do something,* and Angela said no because they had problems with those neighbors. Next Mom asked Angela's then-husband Vito (whose name ironically means "life") to help the dog, and he said no, too. So Mom said she was going to do something about it, and both Angela and Vito told her emphatically to mind her own business.

Mom listened all night in bed to the storm and to the poor dog outside, flailing in the middle of it all. The trip was now tainted.

Being the animal lover she was, Mom was psychologically hurt because she was a saver of lives but could not save this poor dog.

As planned, Mom left the next day (of course looking out the window first to see if the dog was still there, and he wasn't). She hoped that the animal was finally safe inside with his family. It was a couple of weeks before Mom got the nerve to ask her cousin what had happened to the dog. When she finally did, Angela said the dog had died. He was put in a garbage bag and out with the trash. (Did Mom really need to know *all* of that?)

Buried deep inside Mom's mind was something she never forgot. It would be with her for a long time. She literally took a trip to paradise, and something like this happened, which caused the devil to show its face. (Sorry, but more than one devil.) Mom's not mad at Angela, though, because if I hadn't died in that storm, I would not be in Mom's life now.

Huh? Did I just say that?

Mom was driving, once again randomly pondering what the animal communicator had told her. How I had come into this life "with extra baggage" because there were still lessons to be learned due to a life cut short. I was too big. I couldn't hear. I made stones. I never seemed to learn. I was hyper. But my sweet nature redeemed me.

All of a sudden, there was a strike of lightning (not a real one), and Mom thought of the dog in my dream, then of the dog in Hawaii, and put the puzzle together. The dog Mom wanted to help, who had died out in the storm and who had gone to the afterlife, only to come back right away, was me, Dexter! It didn't matter if anyone agreed with her; she knew it deep in her soul, and she finally felt free. She sobbed on the side of the road where she had pulled over. She called the dog whisperer and asked if this were so and was told yes, but it didn't matter to her. This realization freed me. Mom figured it out and put it all together in her mind, something that came through a communicator of animals.

Mom (and I!) then knew who we were, why we were together, what our bond was. It had nothing to do with Dinah in North Royalton and her $1,000 Dalmatians. It explained why I could not get inside fast enough when a storm was brewing, why I didn't even want to go on walks because I hated leashes. The karma between us was finally over in the sense that Mom had finally saved me, and if we were ever separated, I would always be safe in my mom's love. Circumstances may change, like broken marriages, grannies dying, and daughters leaving, but love remains. I was the dog in the storm, and Mom couldn't save me then, so she saved me now.

When it storms outside in the night now, and I am sleeping at the foot of Mom's bed, she reaches to touch me, and we both are grateful to finally be together, all safe and sound. *And finally I settled down and became the good dog I was meant to be!* We had walked over coals together, and we had passed the test.

Everything came back full circle. My life on Maui, the communicator's message, my dream/near-death experience with Getta and Rok—all of it brought us here.

But how did I get from Hawaii to the Croatian hills to here? From a little shepherd dog to a Dalmatian from heaven? Well, we don't always understand everything. Some things remain unknown. There have to be some secrets only the universe knows. The only thing I can say is that we have many dreams, many worlds, different lives and times, and we hopefully remember and dream about the happier ones.

And all I want to do on this earth is *love!*

Oh, by the way, Izzie and I are cool. She is so sweet, but she holds her own. And she is so simple. (Not complicated like me.) She barks what she means and means what she barks, or something like that. "Let the little dogs show us the way." She has a well of love inside her—pure love. Izzie is peaceful. She loves herself. She loves her spot, and she has a couple of big spots.

And I love *her*. Now write that down because you may never hear it again.

# Chapter 22

## THE END

When Granny passed, Mom was at peace because no stones had been left unturned. About six months before, Granny was going downhill, so a day and a half after Mom's birthday, when Granny was eating nothing but had attempted to put the tip of her tongue on cake frosting, she told Granny to please go to heaven because she couldn't bear to see her that way anymore. Well, Granny was very tired, and she passed that night just as Mom had told her to do. She had always said that for anything to just "ask Vickie."

Mom says it is special when a loved one passes on your birthday or a holiday. Granny was just a little late. Four years prior, she went to the nursing home on Mom's birthday. I don't think Granny felt very privileged then because there was no privilege in that. That was the birthday Mom cried in bed all day. She earned it!

At the funeral, there were so many indications that Granny was present in spirit before she went to the light. For one thing, one of the flower arrangements fell down. Mom had planned the Mass, so why not be there? "As long as I shall live, I will testify to love" went the one song.

Another incident that stands out that made us know Granny and other loved ones were there happened on the way to the cemetery: There was a dog in a fenced front yard who looked like Domino. Mom said, "Meg, look at the Dal who looks like Domino."

Meg said, "Mom, look at the dog next to him who looks just like Dice!"

Domino and Dice were all around there, at the funeral, in place with our beloved family. That was comforting.

A couple of months later, Mom called the home and asked the Mother Superior if she had a job for her. Well, that was the beginning of the rest of her life. To paraphrase a song by Susan Boyle: "I am doing what I was born to do."

Mom left Dad but then let him move in with her (in the finished attic) in a house a little down the road. No longer would I have to worry about being abandoned. Things were more secure on the home front. My family all loves me so much, and Izzie says I am hers. Mom and Dad are friends. They are kind to and help each other. They no longer fight.

Love has healed Megan and helped her come of age. I am six now, and Izzie is five. Megan is not in California, Florida, or Chicago but goes to school locally (she gets all A's) and has a job working with autistic children. Mom told her to get a job with meaning; she did, and she loves it. Mom told Meg to always remember that these beautiful souls are here for us; we are not here for them. Their vibration is higher than the earth's, so their spirits are uncomfortable in the physical plane. It's all an evolving process, focusing on the journey itself and not the end of the journey, and there is always time.

Mom's job at the nursing home has transformed her life. She believes that the job was a gift from Granny, and that she was hired by God. Mom also felt she wanted to give back to the home for all it had done for Granny. Mom made a pact with Granny that when she sends her friends over, she is to greet them at the gates.

Mom often works with people who are near the end, and she in essence helps them pass. She never could have done this before Granny died. But Granny's was the ultimate death, so after that, Mom wasn't afraid anymore. She tries to brighten a lot of lives. She looks in the mirror and doesn't even recognize the person looking back at her—so natural in a uniform, so in her element. Not working there would make her feel defrocked. God and Granny are working through her.

Mom feels energy change around a person who is not long for this world. The air turns gray. She knows when a person is between planes, not in heaven yet but slightly out of the world—all natural talents she never knew she had. She has seen a lot of spirits and often hears her name called out, but nobody's there. She always knows it is simply "her people" calling out to her. She has whispers in her ear.

Mom told a lady about the hearts she and Meg saw. (An example of the hearts after Gran passed: Mom was making noodles with a little oil in the pan, and after she washed out the oil, the outline of a heart remained in the pan.) The lady said, "Why, it's the Sacred Heart of Jesus!" Somehow the lady knew that Mom had been through a lot. Mom said she didn't think so. Well, the lady went home for Thanksgiving and said that before the football game came on, she saw a big heart on the screen! She didn't tell her family but thought to herself, *Wow, I'm seeing Vickie's hearts!* The lady passed about a week later, after squeezing Mom's hand while in a coma.

Mom took one lady's shoes after she died and now has flowers in them on the back porch. Mom didn't keep Granny's shoes—it hurt too much—but she kept this lady's. So that's progress.

There was another lady who adopted Mom from the time she got there. The whole time the lady was dying, Mom kept hearing the song lyric, "Sailing takes me away . . . soon I will be free." She told the lady to tell Jesus she was ready after telling her family she loved them. The lady was soon at peace.

Mom works in the dining room of the nursing home and in the activities department, visiting those people who aren't physically able to go to activities. The dining room is actually the Ritz, with its chandeliers and "The Blue Danube" often playing in the background. She often gets remarks like "You ought to get a job at a restaurant where you could get more money."

She answers, "The tips are better here."

But what she really is to these people is their advocate.

Working with the aged, the main thing Mom has learned is this: Now is all there is because life's so unpredictable and short. When you are there with these people, the moment means everything because after you leave, they may not even remember that you were there with their favorite pastry. So never do anything tomorrow. It may be too late. Giving them a little bit of happiness is worth it all! It's not a sad job. Mom is not helping them die but to be born into the next life. For that reason, why shouldn't it be an honor to die on a loved one's birthday?

I told Mom that she should make me her partner. She could do her thing, and I could be a therapy dog! I could even ride with her to work every morning. But mostly these days I am with my dad, bonding. Time will reveal my next move.

Along with Karma, this book has to end, too. But nowadays chapters are really long, so maybe this is just the end of another chapter. There's a whole lot of life ahead for us all, so who's to say there might not be a sequel, or even a full novel, down the road? Granny had said it all: that the story was about to be over, so we run and take a bow in the play of life as the audience says, more, *more*. Then we go out again, and I do something erratic, so Dexter-like, and jump in the lap of the lady in the front row. Her mouth is now open, all aghast!

And God continues to shed His light on us because His spirit takes care of its own. Amen.

End of play, err, book!

And with that, I say it really *is* the end.

*Bliss you!*

*Wild like the wolf*

*Bam!*

# Afterword

August 4, 2015

Hello everyone!

Now that Dexter is gone, I ask myself, *Why was he born into this life for me, with all his problems, and why was it that I wanted and saved and loved him?*

He was a special needs dog, so he needed more. There is something very endearing about that. We were his hearing. He was Izzie's purpose and, while he was at it, kept us all connected. (There were even a couple of small miracles that occurred after he died.) Izzie was his little service dog. She barked (actually wailed) at him outside to protect him because she just couldn't bear for anything to happen to him. If he made her mad, she'd scold him by nibbling his ears or his back end, the most vulnerable parts of him, to keep him in line. She sneaked his bones, and the goober that he was, he let her. Of course Izzie misses him, but we are showering her with extra love. I often see her staring into space at nothing. Maybe it is Dexter. Or she stares at his picture.

Dexter was sick only one week. A squirrel in the backyard that he chased up a tree on a daily basis came on the porch right after he became ill, looking for him. They were friends.

My mother "Granny" wasn't an animal lover, but she always helped me with my dogs because, darn it, it was the right thing to do. So I just know as Dexter transitioned, she was right there to claim him because he is ours.

Some of the Eastern cultures believe that animals were born to us for soul growth and that we will be judged by how we treat them. (They say you can always tell what kind of person someone is by the way he treats his dog.) Animals may be sacred. I believe (from my research and intuition) that when they're attached to humans, they go to a doggie heaven when they pass, across the famous Rainbow Bridge. Sometimes they reincarnate again, if not to be with the same person, then to be with someone in the same family. (They have many lives to one human life, so a person could have about eight dogs in a lifetime! Imagine all those Dexters!) But other times they don't come back. They go to heaven when they are laid to rest and exist in eternity with friends and family. They wait for us and then run free with us on the other side, happy forever. If there was ever a purer being who didn't need to come back for more lessons, it would be Dexter.

I'm sure there are many other reasons locked deep inside as to why we were meant for each other, my soul dog. How about he was a *Magnificent being,* and I was lucky to have him?

I can't know what Dexter is thinking (or do I?)—I have to let him go—but I hope he is in a better place, telling everyone that it was a good ride, the food was great, he had fun, and he adored and felt adored! I sure hope he is not driving everyone nuts up there at the gates, going in and out, in and out (like he used to do here because he didn't want to miss a trick)! But one thing is for sure: There really is no death!

My cell phone was just ringing, and before I could answer it, something slung the phone across the room.

RIP Dexter!

2/24/2007–8/4/2015

Sincerely,

Vickie Versace Mullins

*Dexter in Summerland*

# About The Author

Vickie Versace Mullins is a bubbly spirit who prefers laughing through life rather than all the other alternatives. She has a B.A. in English Literature from Cleveland State University in Cleveland, Ohio. She is a poet, and Dexter's story is her first attempt at prose. She has published poems in various local literary magazines. She lives with her family in Cleveland, Ohio.

CPSIA information can be obtained
at www.ICGtesting.com
Printed in the USA
BVHW050433181218
535676BV00028B/434/P

9 781460 287484